11/98

JL

A New Home for Tiger

A New Home for Tiger

Joan Stimson

Illustrated by
Meg Rutherford

BARRON'S

Look for *Big Panda, Little Panda* and *Swim Polar Bear, Swim!*
also by Joan Stimson and Meg Rutherford.

All inquiries should be addressed to:
Barron's Educational Series, Inc.
250 Wireless Boulevard
Hauppauge, New York 11788

International Standard Book No. 0-7641-0102-1

Library of Congress Catalog Card No. 96-86548

PRINTED IN HONG KONG
9 8 7 6 5 4 3 2 1

Once upon a time there was a cheerful tawny tiger.

He could swim like a fish.
He could eat like a horse.
And each night he slept like a dormouse.

One day at dinner, Mother Tiger
looked excited.
"We're moving, Tiger," she told him.

Then she took Tiger outside and pointed across the lake. "I've found a new house for us and tomorrow we must pack up our things."

Early the next morning Tiger put his toys in a pile. He bounced around Mother and helped load the bundles.

"This *is* fun," he said.

At last they were ready to leave.
A little way down the trail Tiger stopped.
He took a last look at his old house.

"Hurry up, Tiger," called Mother, "or we'll never get there."

By the time they reached the new house, it was almost dark. Tiger padded through the doorway and looked inside.

"It's all different," he whispered after supper.
"Can I sleep in your bed?"
he asked Mother.

That night Tiger tossed and turned.
When he woke up he wasn't sure
where he was. And, when Mother
began to empty the bundles,
Tiger wouldn't help.

"I don't like it here,"
he wailed.
"I want to go home."

Mother explained patiently. "We have a new home now, Tiger." Then she read him his favorite story and gave him a hug.

But Tiger still felt grumpy. He refused to swim in the lake with the other tigers. He began to play with his food instead of eating it.

And night after night he woke Mother.
"*I want to go home,*" he kept telling her.

One day Tiger packed up his things.

"I'm going home now," he announced.
"*This* is our home," explained Mother.

But Tiger had made up his mind.
"If Mother won't take me, then I'll go by myself."

As soon as the moon came up,
Tiger set off.

At first Tiger was excited. "I'm going home. I'm going home," he sang. And he bounced along through the forest.

But, when he reached their old
house, the moon disappeared.
Tiger began to feel uneasy.
He looked nervously over
his shoulder.

Then he padded inside.
"I'm home, I'm home," he whispered
into the empty house.

But home didn't feel right. There was no sound
of Mother humming or snoring. There was no
smell of her warm fur or a tasty meal.
There was no one to tell him a story
or give him a hug.

Tiger felt confused. Then he realized what was wrong. Tiger bounded all the way back through the forest.

Mother Tiger woke with a start.
"Whatever is it?" she asked.
"I want my home!" cried Tiger. *"I want my home!"*

Mother sat up and yawned. "This is our *new* home . . ." she began.

But Tiger wouldn't let her finish.

"I know that now!" he cried. Then he tried to explain.
"There's *no* home left in our old house," said Tiger, *"because
it's all moved here!"*

The next morning a cheerful tawny tiger went out to play. He splashed in the lake with his new friends. "Come to dinner at my house," he told them.

That night Tiger bounced on his bed at bedtime.
"It's time to tuck me in," he shouted to Mother.

But Mother was still cleaning up dinner. And by the
time she came in to Tiger . . . he was sleeping like a
dormouse!